THE HOUSE OF STORI

BOOK ONE THE SECRI

Its a collection of adventures that a young women dreamed that she had undertaken as she slowly built herself a new life.

Once upon a time there was a wonderful small cottage built on the cliff of a small seaside town. Everyone that had lived or visited there experienced the enchantment of the cottage. As in their lives had been victims of sort of emotional problem in their lives before coming to the cottage . And as soon as they came in to the cottage to find that their lives were to change. Rebecca was the first to experience the enchantment of the cottage since the previous owners had died. And needed a new owner or it was going to be bulldozed by property developers. The house was to auctioned and sold within twenty eight days. Rebecca had always dreamt of owning a place of her own . She had viewed over the years many properties that she liked the look of and had been up for sale. So when the cottage on the cliff top had been put up for sale she went straightaway to the estate agent that were selling it on the behalf of the previous owner family. There she asked one of them if she could view it. The answer was Yes but wasn't to go inside the cottage until the day of the auction but she could see inside through the windows.

With every viewing in the past she was able to go inside but it didn't matter as she saw what she could inside through the front window she instantly fell in love with the cottage. She had some savings for her weekly allowance which he received from caring for her new partner. Daniel was Rebecca's new partner, he was some years older than her but it didn't matter to her. He had health problems which meant he need to be cared for daily. Some time it affected his mobility so they didn't get out much. The cottage would give them a fresh start and some happiness to both of them.

She had lost all her friends that she had before the divorce . Only to find new ones that were to be more like family to her than her own. As like true friends they had stood by her when it felt like the world around her was ending . They were always looking for away to show that there was something to be happy about each day. So her visits to Thomas and Diana were a welcome break.As every time Rebecca had visited them after the viewing of the house they noticed how happier she was . All she spoke about was what plans she had dreamt of f she was to get that cottage.

They knew that she had a small amount saved but it wouldn't be enough to buy that cottage within the time allowed. She couldn't even afford to rent it let alone buy it .

She had done so much of them both over the years of friendship since she gotten to know them. Each night they would sit and talk of how they could thank her in some way that would change her life for the better . So a few day before the auction Thomas and Diana had approached the Estate agent and placed a private bid which was immediately accepted. Rebecca had came to visit as she did every week to chat and see if they were ok .

But on this visit she was quiet as a mouse and gloom."What's up pet your not your cheerful self?" Thomas asked her.

"Oh it just that I've heard that the seaside cottage has been sold via a private sale." As tears rolled down her face.

"Well there's always other houses ."

"Not one like that "Seeing that this upset Rebbeca even more Diana change the subject and they drank their three pm cuppas . Which were followed by ham and peas pudding sandwiches with cake.

Diana had earlier in the day had baked the cake by her own recipe. Putting down the tray with the teapot and cups on the coffee table so Rebbeca could serve the tea. As she had to bring the other tray through with the cake and sandwiches on. When Diana was settled in her seat Rebecca poured the teas into each cup and handed them to Thomas and Diana. After they finished this Rebbeca helped Diana do the dishes then Kissed and cuddled both her friends and went home to her partner. When the keys and deed arrived the following day they were over the moon that they were helping a friend change her life. So they had to arrange for away to give Rebbeca the keys and deeds.

"Thomas what if I phone her and ask if she could come round today instead of her usual day ?"

"Yeah she might go for that go ahead ." Diana picked up the phone dialled Rebecca's phone number and waited .

"Hello "

"Hello rebbeca its Diana here are you doing anything at three pm today as we would like you to visit us then instead of your normal time ."

"Ive got nothing on at three pm but why do you want me to see today instead of tomorrow ."

"Oh just thought it would be a nice change and we need to speak to you?"

"Ok see you then." Diana put the phone down after saying bye for now.But on the other end Rebbeca wondered what was so important that Diana had to ring. Looking forward into seeing her friend she wondered if it was Thomas health getting worse or something else that made Diana ring her to rearrange her visit . As Rebecca rang the doorbell at three pm Diana opened their front door to Rebecca and gave her a hug before they headed towards the sitting room. Thomas was sitting in his high backed armchair.

As usual she asked how he was."Well the best one can do in my situation pet."

Diana had at this time left the room to get the tea ready. It was alway a light one as Thomas couldn't eat large meals any more since he had his major heart attack some years ago.

"How have you being doing and hows Daniel these days?"

"I'm ok but Daniel has been poorly at late. But we have to just get on with life the best we can ."

"Thomas don't you have an envelope to give Rebbeca !" Still in the kitchen making the tea as Rebecca was about to take a seat on their sofa in the sitting room .

"Here take this ."

"Diana what's in it?"

"Well Rebecca pet open it and see ."As she entered the room carrying a tray with cake on.

Rebbeca get hold of the envelope after putting Thomas's cup down on the table next to his chair and returned to her seat to tear open the envelope and pours it into her lap. "Keys what for ?"

"Well look to see what else is in there."Gently Rebecca pulls out a folded piece of paper she started to unfold it.

"What is this real?"

"Yes they are the key and deeds in your name pet for that cottage by the sea.

"But why ?"

"Rebbeca because you deserve it after everything you have been through these past years" Thomas answered. Diana and Thomas had not been away for a few years as they couldn't afford to but had saved up to go away in a few months time but had decided to use it to buy the cottage for Rebecca . "Diana I had thought you were saving for that holiday? "

"Yes but we thought we could always come and stay with you for a holiday."On that Rebecca got up and hugged both of them with tears of happiness falling down her face. Once tea had finished and had done the dish with Diana she then left them to go home .

Rebecca arrived home and told him what they had done. Agreed after talking with Daniel. They had planned for her to get the new house ready to live in before he was to arrive there a few days later.She had packed a few of the essentials and some of their small things into boxes that night. Taking them with her the following morning in a taxi. As she couldn't carry them her self on the bus. Rebecca reached the house at midday. Got out of the taxi and lifted the all the boxes one at a time onto the first step of the porch of the house before the driver drove away after she had paid him. Rebecca took out the keys from her coat pocket and opened the door, then lifted the first box up top carry through it. She didn't stop till all the boxes where through the door placing each on within the doorway. Pushing them forward enough to close the door behind her suddenly things felt different . Somehow the enchantment of the house had woken from the deep sleep as the light went on without her touching them.

This she just thought that the lights must be those connected to sensor under the carpet which once they pick up the weight change on pressure pads switched on as you entered a room. So she wasn't shocked. But it was the enchantment the house that had switched them on. She had wanted to get started on unpacking straight way as it would let her get to know each room as she hadn't been able to seen inside of her viewing.

The first box to unpack was ornament that her and Daniel had brought together in the first year together. She wanted them to me on show in the sitting room. Looking at each door trying to work out what was behind them. She looked to her left and turned the handle gently then pushed with her hand till it was wide enough to carry the box through. Picking the box up she notice a beautiful carved mantel piece covered with dust. It would be perfect for her things once dusted. She had small duster in the box which she pulled out once she had placed it near the mantel piece. Slowly and gently she rubbed each of the mantels carved figures and place one item out of the box . The figure suddenly started to slowly move to show a small door. It was also carved but with more intricately carved with spring images. With this she wondered what secret it may be hiding behind. Rebecca couldn't stop herself from touching the handle to see if it opened. As she touched it opened the wonderful smell of daffodils and sweet roses wafted through. As it had opened wider over a few moments a sight of a young deer in the field ahead of her appeared. The daffodils grew along the edge of the field which had a path near it. Stepping onto the path she felt the sun lightly touch her face. It was peaceful and made her want to keep on walking to see if she was alone or if there was anything else to see. Putting her foot door to make her next step further along the path she thought "Well if this it real I should be able to touch those daffodils. "

"HELLO REBECCA"

"Who's that calling my name ?"

"Me come and Look for me?"

"How I am I supposed to look for you when I can't even see you ?"

"Follow my voice !" She followed the voice across a field to a small flowering bush . Being careful not to trample on and of the wild flowers that were hiding behind the daffodils.

"OVER HERE ." As Rebecca looked at the bush there was a small spring sprite sitting on the branch at the top near a budding rose. Waiting to be spotted she was shaking her head till the eyes of Rebecca fell on to her .

"Hello you've found me my name is Dawnfire."

"How do you know my name ?"

"I just know !" In a huff as though some certain person had just offended her intelligence.

"Just wondering and sorry if I,ve offended you by asking you."

"Ok I will forgive you this time I might now the next time."

Rebecca looked around then asked Dawnfire "Where am I ?"

"Oh don't you know you've entered my enchanted world but don't worry you're still in your house as well."

"But how can I be in two places?"

"Well that a story I can tell you if you would like to hear it ?"

"Yes please Dawnfire "

"OK sit down carefully on the grass and I'll fly down to you and sit on your knee ." So Rebecca sat down softly on the grass as soon as she was comfortable Dawnfire flew down onto her knee.

"Well many thousands of years in my time long before your cottage was built there was a great house where your cottage is now. Which a kind family lived in till illness took them and they died. On that day a enchantment was somehow placed on the house all that was in it which also included all of us imagined creatures that the children had dreamt of in their lifetime . Other members of the external family had tried to live in the great house but had wanted to change the place so much to their liking. By hiding the beautiful carvings and paintings behind other things like the way they had hid the doorway you came through. Which had been losted till you found it ."

"But why me ?"

We know that you can see beauty and goodness in other that others can't."

"But what if I wanted to do the same as the others to the house?"

"Look at the way you gently rubbed the mantel figures to clean them."

"Yes I did that so I wouldn,t damage them."

"But as you rubbed didn't you sense there was some beauty in them beneath the dust ?"

"Yes the way they had been carved ."

"Well that show you that your have the ability to find beauty in things you see or touch ."

"OK Dawnfire I see your point ."

"By you being able to find the beauty you will be able find all the other carved items and releasing their stories. Those stories were those that the children had made up to give life to the carvings but also gave each of the enchanted creature's life in their dreams.

"So as I clean the cottage up I will find the other carved items and release the stories like the door was first one and it represented spring which is why everything you see if of spring around us. So this must be your story Dawnfire and your must be to my guess be a spring sprite that help mother nature ."

"Yes Rebecca I am and would you like to see some of the thing we help her with?"

"Yes please but im huge compared to you ."

"OPPPS I forgotten about that!"

But as soon as Dawnfire had said opphs Rebecca had shrunk to the same size and tapped her on her shoulder . "Am I the right size now?"

"As I said you can see beauty in everything even the smallest things."

"Ok where are we going ?"

"Well I think we will take a flight to see how good the buttercups are this year." On that Dawnfire Rebecca's hand and off they flew towards the the buttercups.some of the other spring sprites were sprinkling gold dust over the butter cups.

"So that why as a child when we picked a buttercup and put it under our chins it shone if we liked butter it looked golden. "

"But Rebbeca every buttercup you picked cut down the amount of nectar that the poor worker bees could collect to take back to the hive to make that delicious honey that the beekeeper collect and put into the jars which you buy and enjoy you enjoy on your toast in the morning . And there will be less flowers for the cows to munch on to produce the milk and butter "

"I've never thought of that."

"Has that made you think about changing your action and what the impacts that they have nature.Possibly make you stop picking too many of them when they appear in the spring."

"OH yes as I love my honey and butter ."

"Dawnfire had started to tire so the flew of to a primrose .

Rebecca had gotten worried for her new friend so asked " Are you ok Dawnfire?"

"Yes I,m just tried from my flying around like that as it sometime does that to me after awhile."

"Well if you tell how to get back to my world I'll go and let you rest up."

" Ok that easy just have to move your hand as though you're still cleaning the mantel and your will find yourself back there. "

"Bye for now Dawnfire. as she started to move her hand as though she was dusting the mantel piece. The smell of beeswax hit the back of her nose as she realized that she was back in her sitting room.Putting her last ornament onto the mantel with a smile of pleasure of achieving a goal.  Her stomach had started rubble tell her it was time she had some lunch. Her second box was still in the passage in it was some groceries and other kitchen stuff. So picked it up and walked straight down the passage to the kitchen door. Entering the kitchen she put the box on the bench then took her kettle out and put it on. got out the bread and sandwich stuff out of the box as she looked  for the cupboards to put the rest of the things away when she saw there was a larder. "I wonder if there is anything init

?" She asked herself in her head as she was still alone in the house. So opening the larder door and looked in. On the first shelf she saw was a pot of pure honey. She walked to take a closer look at it. It wasn't opened and looked brand newso she took it back to the bench where she was about to make a sandwich and spread some on the slice of bread for a honey sandwich. The kettle boiled so she made her cuppa .

Drinking her cuppa and eating her sandwich she thought of her next job she need to get done if she was to have it ready for Daniels arrival in two days time. Knowing the if she got behind in the tasks she need doing today it meant that it would be a late night for her. Soon as she had finished her lunch she went back to the sitting room to get on with cleaning the windows. Which was to be a task and a half as they had not been cleaned in many years. She tried rubbing them with the cloth but not even that made a mark through the amount of dust and grime on them. Remembering the way her grandmother had told her that they used to use vinegar and old newspaper. Having plenty of the newspaper in the box that the ornaments had been wrapped in. But the vinegar was in the kitchen so off she head back to the kitchen to get it.

She was only half way there when "Wind up the Cuckoo Clock Rebecca."

"Dawnfire is that you?"

" Yes please can you wind up the Cuckoo Clock with the key behind the pendulum ."Quickly Rebecca found the key and wound the clock up with the clock fully wound up it seem to come back to life as the cogs inside ticked and tocked . But the little carved wooden Cuckoo that had been stuck in on position due to the clock needing winding suddenly came alive and to Rebecca's surprise spoke to her.

"Cuckoo Cuckoo hello " the wooden cuckoo spoken.

"Was that you just said hello " as looked at the clock to see if it was the Cuckoo .

"Yes I'm the one that said hello."

"Am I to help you like I hoped Dawnfire."

"Yes please if you can as the door on my clock house are stuck and I've been stuck here for along not able to rest at all, the only way to open them is if you can help is give a little whistle ."

"Well I can only but give it a try." Rebecca pursed her lips and whistled and the doors of the clock opened. But to the ears of Rebecca she couldn't hear a sound coming out of her mouth. Yes it must of been a whistle sound as the door on the clock opened slowly.

"Thank you is there anyway I can help you return ?"

"Yes how can I get back to Dawnfire."

"Close your eyes and turn the key once more you will be back at her side."

"Thankyou and I will remember to wind your clock up daily ."

"Thank You Rebecca." On closing with the key still in it hole she turned it once more and she was right there next to Dawnfire . As soon as she was in Dawnfire sight the little sprite had wanted to know if Rebecca had enjoyed her gift.

"Did you enjoy your honey ?"

"Yes thank you where did it come from ?"

"The Bees sent it to say thankyou for not picking the buttercups in the field you crossed earlier."

" Could you not wind the cuckoo clock up from here?"

"No as Cuckoo is from your side of the carving so I'm grateful that you helped her out." For that I'm going to show you something secret and special to all of us enchanted creature but I will have to ask you to promise that you will only use what you see in times of danger or to help others. "

"I promise." Dawnfire spun around twice then stopped reaching out her hand and grabbed hold of a spiders web strand pulled gently . The spider came to where they both were standing.

"Jump On !" Both had gotten on the spider without any problems. Dawnfire gently tapped her feet on either side of the spider as it started to climb up its web. It got half way up when Dawnfire kicked a strand of the web and it stopped . They quickly dismounted and the spider went on its way thinking there was a big fly trapped in it web ready to be eaten. Where had they stopped? Well it was were the web had caught a leaf of blue bell for support . But the leaf also gave shelter to the elves that had collected the tiniest pieces of fallen stars.

"Shhh look down there."

"Whats up?"

"Look and see down there and you will see that secret I was talking about ." she whispered. It was a elf putting the tininess pieces of fallen stars into a pot. The glow of the stars shone as bright as the buttercups. "But why are they collecting the pieces?"

"Its for when we are in danger ."

"But why store it like that?" as the elf was putting it into a hole in a oak tree.

"Oh it like our version of what the irish pixies do with their pot of gold at the end of the rainbow."

"Oh so to stored away so other people like me don't get to misuse it."

"So that why its also a secret and we only know of it and use it to freeze those that are hurting others sprites . Sometimes use some of it to help us when we send happy dreams to your world at night time if there are people like you that are sad."

"Wow that how my dreams have been good lately but I thought they were all from the bfgs world."

"No hes just our cover story as he helps to tidy up all the dreams for reuse. Anyway we better go before someone realises we have been watching." As Quickly as the click of Dawnfires fingers they had moved somewhere else. "You must have trusted me for you to show me that?" sensing how important the trust was in this situation .

"Yes and you're also the first person from the other side of the carvings that I've met."

"But surely you would have met the children that dreamt you all up?"

"No as they couldn't visit ."

"Cuckoo Cuckoo!!!!"

Rebecca shouted as the worker bees had finished gathering the nectar for the honey flew just above them. As the last one pasted over it went quietly again.

"Yes Cuckoo would of seen them everyday as they walked by or looked at him to find the time of day."

Pausing to think Dawnfire though then said "I think there are even stories which Cuckoo is mentioned which both adults and children have read in your world ."

"But why are there so many enchanted creature, people hid in the carvings etc?"

"Because like in the story of Pinocchio Who was granted a wish to be a real live boy but broken his promise to the blue fairy that he would be good , well that made all of us enchanted creatures and people to decide to only show ourselves to those that have prove that they could be trusted by their actions."

At this Rebbeca realised that she had also made a promise on the mobile phone to keep him updated and also promised to Daniel to have the house ready before he was to arrive which was a few days away , as he had something to sort out. So she said her goodbye for now to Dawnfire and moved her hand as though she was still cleaning, and she was back cleaning the windows.

"Cuckoo Cuckoo" It must be six o'clock and she had just finished the windows just as a new moon was starting to shine through them. There was blankets over the sofa and a open fire which she lit. Got herself comfortable and fell asleep on the sofa with the blanket wrapped round her. Early the following morning as the Cuckoo Clock cuckooed it was six am she woke up feeling happy at the thought of what the day could bring. Adventures that ahead of her were to come throughout the day. To the kitchen she went and made her first cup of tea of the day then finished unpacking the kitchen stuff. Putting all the tins on the top shelf in the larder. Then her dried s food including flour also bread on the but the fresh bread on the middle shelf with the cottage being an old one that it might have mice. All the cleaning stuff on the bottom shelf as she could reach it. Keeping hold of a duster and some beeswax went to find the bedrooms. Heading along the passage she found the stairwell with a wooden handrail rubbing it with a little bit a beeswax that was left on the duster as she climbed the stairs gently treading on each step.

As she didn't know if they were still solid enough . Looking at the condition of the walls and saw that all they had some money in their bank account. which they could do themselves when Daniel arrived.

At the top of the stairs there was three doors one to her left , one to her right , one to the front of her. she picked the door to her left as she thought that this could become their bedroom. Once she had cleaned it ready for the rest of her furniture to arrive. But it also meant that she had somewhere to sleep tonight. And sleep comfortably in a bed if there was one in that room. Quickly turning the porcelain handle the door opened. She thought it would be cold to the touch no it was warm as her hand wrapped round it to turn it. To her delight there was the most beautiful carved bedroom set in front of her in that room hidden under dust sheets as she slowly lifted each one. The first was a dressing table and stool in front of the window. like the mantel down stairs it was in need of a clean so she got her duster and rubbed the mirror first till she not only saw her reflection but another face also there. but it vanished as quickly as it had appeared in it. Surely it wasn't a ghost that she saw in the mirror but a picture that was hanging behind her she thought. Turning around to look to see if there was a picture hanging with that same face on it not one in sight . She took her duster and continued to clean the dresser. Opening ever little draw and rubbed them with bees wax, then did the same on the larger ones. As she opened the first one out popped a secret draw in it was a locket and key with a note.

Whom finds this will release me as seen in the picture in the locket. But I will not take you to the places where my story but with the key you will be able to go there yourself. As I will be able to join the rest of my family who are waiting in heaven for me to join them . with my thanks & God Bless You. Marcus Of wishing Well. She had Just put them into her pocket when she heard the voice of her friend Diana shouting at the bottom of her stairs.

"Rebbeca where are you?"

"I'm upstairs in the front bedroom!"

They had came to see how she was getting on with the new house.

"Stay there Im coming down."

So down the stairs she went to see her friends, hugging both of them as soon as she saw them.

"Come through to the kitchen and I made us some tea." Diana had carried a small box through with her in it was her wonderful cakes. Thomas sat at the small table he, which had took the sheet off.

"Well what have you been upto since your arrival Rebecca?"

" I've done the sitting room and found a wonderful carved mantel piece like those that are in those big medieval national trust houses but it has shelves on it. "

"So you will be doing the bedrooms this morning. "

"Yes thats why I was upstairs when you shouted ."

"Well while we're here and have a bit time on our hand I could give you a helping hand if you would like that?"

" OH yes please as it would mean I'd get them finished before tea time but only if you want to Diana . Thomas if you want you can go into the sitting room and sit in there while we girls get some more of the work done."

"OK as I will be able to read the newspaper I've brought with me ." which he proceeds to pull from his coat pocket .

They walked to the sitting room with him then went up stairs Rebecca shown her what she found. Then started to take the sheets of the rest of the furniture that the previous owners had left behind. On finding a bed under one they stripped all the bedding of it. All that was wrong with the bedding was that it all needed washing then could be put back onto the bed. In The last box Rebecca had brought to the house was some of her best bedding so she sent Diana downstairs to fetch it as she finished removing all the bedding.

Just as Diana had got back into the bedroom Rebecca noticed something. " Diana whats this ?"

A chest at the bottom of the bed which was locked. "Hang on that key might open it." Diana told her.

Putting in the key into the lock on the chest it opened and there was her surprise fresh sheets and blankets full works.

"But look at them it as though he previous owners have thought of everything that you could need all look brand new ."

"Its as they have left little gifts everywhere and I wonder what's in the next room."

" But what should I do with these then." They put the new bedding on the bed and it looked regal then left to the next room. It was similar as there was another bedroom set hid under the sheets. But the bedding was in better condition .

"All that this room need is some light I think." so Rebecca walked towards a window and opened the curtains and the light streamed in. AS it hit the bed Diana froze for a moment but was able to speak still.

"Rebecca I sense that we are doing the right thing here ."

"I know I can sense it too."

"Diana its time we went as we've got shopping to do.

"Ok Im coming."

" By the way do you need anything that we can get you from the shops."

"Yes just the basic's as tomorrow hopefully I will be finished and be able to go and collect the rest of our stuff and of course get Daniel."

"OK will do and don't worry about paying us back!"

On the two of them hugging they went down the stairs saying "See you later." As they left Rebecca's Rebecca thought it would be her chance to take a break for a few minutes from the cleaning. So headed down stairs to the kitchen and looked around noticing that the back door was clean so she opened it and the sea air wafted through. This made her want to sit outside for a bit. She made a cold drink of lemon

tea and went out the door. Sun felt like the ones she had felt in the summer of her childhood. It warmed her body. There was singing coming from somewhere ahead of her. But in her experience she knew that if who ever was singing wanted to be seen they would in their own time come into her own vision.

So she enjoyed her drink of lemon tea slowly. "Sun has his hat on hip hip hora the sun has his hat on summers here so come and play." Then silence as a young man approached her "Sorry am have I disturbed you with my singing mam!"

As though she was royalty. "No and you don't have to call me mem as I'm just Rebbeca."

"Sorry Rebecca I'm Jacob the gardener or used to be before the enchantment of the old place happened ."

" I know all about the enchantment and how it came about as dawnfire has told me all about it."

"She's a quick worker for a spring sprite she is."

"But how comes I've released you as your not a carving as the door I opened was a normal white door."

"Ah but you brought sunshine to my ladies room which had been dark all these years since she passed."

"Do you mean the small room which has cheerful colours in the curtains why yes?"

"Well all I did was open the curtains."

"Then I was released to look after my plants and to see to other tasks. But I haven't yet rewarded you for what you have done. So ask anyway for what you want to see."

She thought awhile for what she would ask for . "Jacob I ask that your able to rest in peace here in your garden as the garden that you know is no longer here but I will try to create a garden that you would have been beyond pleased to have worked in your lifetime if that is what you would like me to do."

"If that is what you wish so be it as for the gardening bit at the corner of the garden you will find my old potting shed to open it just tap gently below the handle and the door will open in here you will find tools and books that will help you." He paused as to think if he could just trust her totally she would be able to finish what he had started all those years ago.

" Rebecca did my Master Marcus leave a key ?"

"Yes why ?"

"Know matter what don't let go of it as it has special powers."

"What do you mean Jacob?"

"With that key as you enter my old potting shed you will find it frozen and as you have the key you will be able to take things from there that I have left behind such as my gardening diary which have secret messages in."

"So I will be able to read those messages."

"Yes and as you do the garden that I started to create for my ladies daughter to enjoy but she never was able to see it as I had not been able to bring myself to finish it before the illness took her."

"I will do my best then ." On that Jacob started to sing again but it was a rhyme she had never heard before " SPRING HAS SPRUNG THE GRASS HAS RAISE ,BIRDS ARE ON THE WING , BUT THATS ABSORBED THE WINGS UPON THE BIRD. As it got quieter as he walked further into the distant. Rebecca felt a little bit sad that Jacob had gone but quickly realised she still only had the rest of the day to finish cleaning. "Rebecca we're back do you want the shopping in the kitchen yet."

As Diana entered the kitchen "Yes please and thanks I'll put the kettle back on if you and Thomas are staying bit longer ?"

"Sorry Rebecca you'll have to make it for yourself as we have got to get ours back as its mostly frozen things. But we'll pop in next week to see how well Daniel has settled in if that ok with you?"

"OF course its ok ,see you to the door ." gave her a kiss as she was leaving the kitchen to take diana to the front door to wave them off. As soon as they drove out of sight she shut the door behind her. Cuckoo cuckoo is it that time again thank you cuckoo .

"Good morning Rebecca"

"How are you today my wooden friend."

"I'm Ok but I sense you're both sad and hungry."

" Yes dear cuckoo your right on both accounts. but right now I can't stop but will do in a bit I just want to see what's behind that door in the kitchen that I spotted as I hope its a bathroom. "

"Ok Rebecca speak to you then cuckoo"

With that she headed to the door she saw and turned the handle which opened easily . To her delight what she found was a beautiful delphine tiled bathroom . The wash basin was a elegant oyster shaped bowl also a pearl white porcelain toilet , but what surprised her the most was the sunken bath that had a the ability to be turned into a spa bath. Looking for where they previous owner would stored their bath towels she spotted a cupboard next to the wash basin. Opening it thinking that there would be nothing in it but found it full of egyptian cotton bath towel in perfect condition that they could of just been bought and placed there only moments ago. As they smelt warm as though they had been dried over hot pipes. She shook her head and nipped her arm to see if she was just dreaming all this. As she look to her arm where she nipped it was red and it was hurting so it wasn't a dream. "We must find out who are leaving these things."She thought to herself. But Thomas had been left down stairs while Rebecca and Diana while they were upstairs earlier on so could it of been him.

"Oh great I will be able to have a long soak before going to bed tonight."as she had just said that out loud to herself she sensed that she wasn't alone. So she headed to the bathroom door to leave when a voice said " Sister I wonder if shes trying to figure out how thing she needs keep on appearing ?"

"I wonder if she's grateful for them ?"a second voice spoke .

"Hello who ever is there please don't be scared to show yourselves I want to thank you ."

Slowly from the corner of her eye appeared two young girls in house maids outfit "Hello mam ."

The one nearest to her replied. Rebbeca then asked "What's your names?"

"I'm Pearl and thats my big sister Ruby" said the smallest girl.

"Pearl you know that your not suppose to speak to the ladies of the house except when spoken to and only to reply yes and no mam. "

"But Ruby I'm not the lady of the house , So you can stop calling me mam and before I forget was it you two that left the gifts around my cottage ."

"Yes but if we not to call you mom what's your name?"

" I'm Rebecca and you know that with me being the owner of the cottage you're no longer servants to anyone here so you can both go free to leave if you wish."

"No No we are happy here and wouldn't know where to go !!" both of them cried in distress.

Rebecca felt that they had only wanted to help her in a way that they only could with them no longer being alive but their spirits had been caught in the enchantment of the cottage. She couldn't bring herself to tell them that they were both dead so decided they could stay. "Well You both have been so thoughtful with your gifts I think I will let you both stay but you have to promise that you don't show your selves to anyone other than me after you have helped my clean this place up ready for my partner to arrive.But you can have the freedom of the cottage and garden .

"Thank You Rebecca ."

" What room needs to be cleaned now"Pearl asked.

" ITs the last room in this cottage its to the right of the top of the stairs as I've not looked into it yet."

"Rebbeca you just open it and we will sort that one out for you."

"THANK YOU PEARL,RUBY." She opened the door but it wasn't a bedroom but a study with shelves full of books that the children would of read against the wall and a table and chair up against a small window . The table was unusual as it had shelfs in the legs with craft items stored in it.

"WOW THIS BEYOND MY DREAMS ."

"Can we stay in this room Rebbeca when your partner is around pleases."Pearl beged

"She'll not want that little sis !"

"Please Rebbeca we'll keep it tidy ?"

"Ok as you need somewhere to stay and you both can help me when I'm creating my cards I like to make if you're in here."

"THANKYOU " Ruby said with a slight sound of happiness that they had finally found a home." And they vanished from her sight. She had taken her back down stairs she could hear the cuckoo clock telling her that it was time she should have something to eat. "Well I should also wind it up as I promise before making myself some tea." so headed to the the clock.

"Hello again Rebecca do you have time now ?"

"Yes my little friend I have a few moments "

"Well get hold of my perch for a second.

"WHY?"

"You will see in a moment !" as she was standing next to the cuckoo.

"Come on into my clock house as I'm having my dinner alone and wish for you to join me as I've got plenty. On entering the clock she notice that the table and chairs were made from the apart of the clock working. "Take a seat." With that she sat down on a cog that tucked under a larger gear that acted like table.

On the table there was a meal and a half on plates which she could choose from such as fly cake or bloodworm rolls . To her they reminded her of the sausage rolls and currant slices her grandmother used to make for her."Oh you must be getting thirsty my friend if so just lift one of those acorn cups and take a sip."

"This tastes delightful what is it?"paused as she took another sip from the cup "Cuckoo it tastes like my favorite soft drink dandelion and burdock."

"You guessed right it is just that." They finished their dinner and Rebecca politely thanked cuckoo.

"Now will you tell me why you're still so sad."

"Oh that garden I can remember hearing of Jacob talking about how beautiful it was going to be once completed and in bloom."

"He's asked me to complete it."

"Dawnfire will be able to help you if you ask her?"

"Thanks for telling me that as your right she could help you as she is a spring sprite."

"I've got let you go as you have so much more work to do."

"Good bye Cuckoo." As quickly as the words had left her mouth she was back in the passage facing the door to the right of the front door. Pushing it open to find a beautiful dining room with a open fire so when xmas came or the weather was bad she could light it and they would still be warm. The larger dining table had a dust sheet over it like the other rooms furniture . Getting hold of two of the corners she pulled it off and found time had protected the table to. As she looked around the room she noticed that there was a beautiful carved cabinet with servers on it. All that was needed was a quick duster. So she folded up all the sheets up she sorted out which were good enough to use on the bed or as the dust sheets when they painted the walls. AS she pull the best ones into the cabinet she placed the others into the boxes that she had emptied.

"Dawnfire," she whispered "where are you?"

"Right here on your mantelpiece."

"I want to ask for your help when I start doing the garden."

" Of course I will as it would give us another way to meet you." with that Rebecca went upstairs to the first bedroom as she had started to feel sleepy . There she folded back the bedding ready to climb into her new bed.

"Good night she whisper ." As her head hit the pillow. But this didn't stop the enchantment of the cottage from coming alive while she slept.

THe phone rang three times then rang off . It was the phone call from her friends to let her know that their arrangements they had for her visit was still ok. So she got up and went to the bathroom to wash after she kissed Daniel on his head to say good morning as he lay still soundly asleep in bed even after the rough night he had . But she felt good about her life. With the only question on her mind being had she dreaming of her future life with Daniel in her sleep but that's another story..............................


## BOOK TWO THE GRANTED WISHES

Story so far

THe phone rang three times then rang off . It was the phone call from her friends to let her know that her visit was still ok. Got up and went to the bathroom to wash and get dressed. Afterwards kissed Daniel on his head to say good morning. As he lay still soundly asleep in bed. Even after the rough night he had . Feeling good about her life,with the only one question on her mind. Had she been dreaming of her future life with Daniel in her sleep but thats is another story.............................

Chapter one Granted wish

It was Thursday morning and her weekly visit to see her good friends. Who treat her more as a daughter as they had no children of their own. She always looked forward to seeing them, as it gave her a break from caring for Daniel. On many occasions over the years she arranged them to receive the extra help they needed. So when they heard about her partner Daniel health problem they want to help her. They had recently came into some money which gave them the opportunity to do something that would help her in the long term. The money was from some premium bonds they had been give the year they had married. As their premium bond numbers had been draw that year. It was a large cash prize enough to buy a house. Rebecca had spoken of her childhood regular when they spoke of the seaside. This gave them the idea of buying a seaside cottage. Diana and Rebecca would sometime go on trips to the seaside by themselves leaving their partners behind. One on trip Diana had looked into a estate agents window. To see if there had been any holiday rental properties that they could rent during the summer as a surprise for Thomas. Little to Rebecca's knowledge this was only an excuse. She had been looking for at the properties that were for sale. One caught her attention a small cottage on the cliff of the seaside town they had visited. When they got back from the trip they spoke of how good the day had been . Rebecca noticed it was getting late so headed home to Daniel. Who was in capable hand of a good friend that lived close to them . Diana saw her to the door thanking her for going with her .

As the year had been tough for both women as they had full time task of caring for their partners. Diana took out of her handbag the details of the property to show Thomas. As soon as he saw it her knew that it would be perfect for Rebecca and her partner Daniel. "Diana does she have any idea on what you were up to?"

"Thomas all she knows is that I was looking for a holiday property that we could rent in the summer."

"Did she see these?"

"Nah Nah as the details were in an envelope."

"So far so good."

"But we have to tell her sometime."

"We will as soon as we have brought that cottage."

"Are You saying that we buy it and put it in her name."

"Yes so get on that barn phone to the estate agent." Diana nervously rings the estate agent. To place her private bid on the cottage. Letting the phone ring twice. "Hello this is Mrs Spencer who asked for the detail on the cliff top cottage."

"Yes hello you're speaking to Davidson and I'm the agent dealing with the salle of cliff top cottage. How may I help you?"

"I've spoken to my husband and we would like to place a private bid on it. But the deeds are to be in the name of Mrs R. Bellado."

"Are you sure you know what that means if we do that ?"

"Yes as Mrs R. Bellado is a friends of our that we are purchasing the cottage for."

"OH I see . Would you want the property taken off the market straight away if your bid is accepted?"

"Yes please and can you also ring us to let us know that its been accepted. The purchase will be complete within the 28 days as we have the money already."

"Ok Mrs Spencer leave that with me." Then put the phone down.

"Thomas thats done and we should hear soon."

"OK pet." The couple knew exactly what they were up to when they started down the route of buying that cottage.

Chapter two Unlocking secrets.

They had been helped over the years by Rebbeca this time they were to help her. Not knowing that there was more than friendship that had brought them together all those years ago. They had been connected by their family histories. Through the generations the story of a Marcus of Wishing Well by Rebecca's family. Her grandmother had told the story to Rebecca throughout her childhood. So when of age to ask questions she wondered if the story had really been of her family history or was it just another fairy tale?"

Even had asked her grandmother that same question. The only answer her grandmother could give her was " Darling Rebecca I wish I knew the answer but the story I've told you all these years is the same one that my own grandmother your great great great grandmother had told me. I've always thought it was only a fairy tale."

But surely then there must been some truth behind the story if its been handed down Rebbeca thought .

"Is there a way that I could find the answer we both look for grandmother?"

"There might be but not from the family as all those that did know the answer possibly are now dead."

So when Rebecca's friend gave the keys and deeds to the cottage had started to unlock the secrets that the family had been keeping within the story. She wasn't dreaming the dream anymore now that the cottage was hers. A lot of cleaning was need to be done within the cottage before Daniel could move into the cottage. As he already had a breathing problem. So had took a full week of hard work and many late nights. Daniel was to arrive at noon today with the furniture van that carried the rest of their things. Soon enough they would be able to relax and start their new life. But suddenly they thought " What was she going to feed Daniel when he arrived as she had not shopping in ." Picked up her mobile phone dial her friends number . " Hi Diana I'm wondering if you could help me ?"

" Of course Rebbeca how can we help ?"

" Daniels arriving at 12 and I've not been able to do any shopping as yet so we've got no food for lunch ."

"Leave it in our hands and well even drop it off at the cottage as it will give us a perfect excuse to visit."

"Thanks you're a life saver."

"We'll be there at 11 and don't worry about paying us back."

"Ok see you then." Already ten am Rebecca had not yet dressed and she needed to get things sorted. The mobile phone rang,"Good morning Rebecca "

"Good morning Darling how's thing your end,briliant I'll be with at 12 as the vans already packed. Ians the driver hes going to drop me and our thing with you then head back."

"Hey have you paid him yet?"

"No as I thought I'll pay him when we reach you."

"Good idea , Oh Dia and tom are coming over with some supplies as I've not be shopping as yet. They will arrive at 11 so we'll have two extra hand to help unpack the van then I'll put a dinner on."

"Perfect see you when I arrive."

"See you." Running up the stairs to the bedroom to finish of getting dressed. Brushing her hair in front of the dressing table mirror. Her eyes caught a glimpse of something or someone behind her. The face was the same one she had seen in her dreams. As soon as she dressed headed back down the stairs. Went to that kitchen and made her morning cup of tea. She was just about to sit down to drink it when the doorbell rang. Clocking up at the clock she see that it was 11,rushes to the front door.

It was Diana and thomas baring gifts bit it still felt strange to hear a doorbell ring. "Brilliant thanks you two!"

"Rebbeca don't even think of paying us back."

"This lot would of cost you a small fortune though ."

"NAH"

"Well you two must same for dinner them as my way to thank you ."

"Ok since you're offering ."

"It would also allow us to see what you've been up to."

Many of the clifftop cottages had been know to have secret passages built into them. As the smugglers would have used the passageways to escape the customs and exercise people or to bring the goods they are smuggling into the country. This had stirred an interest in what inside the cottage looked like, and if their young friend had found anything while cleaning the cottage."Have you not found anything interesting while cleaning up?"

"What like Thomas ?"

"Like hidden doors."

" Why do you ask?"

" Well don't they say that many of the cottages along the coast had hidden smugglers passages."

"Well sorry but I've not found one yet but have seen something in my bedroom dressing table mirror this morning."

"Rebecca lass don't leave us in suspense?"

"A face of a Man."

"You've just been missing Daniel too much."

"Or it could be an imaginary lover."

"HA HA THOMAS ."

"Hes just pulling your leg pet." As he alway enjoyed a good joke. "I know but how have you been able to put up with his jokes so long?"They all just bursted out laughing.

"Pet go and put that kettle on and we'll have a hot cuppa as I'm parched."

"Ok Rebecca where's your kettle?"

" On the bench you will also find there tea,coffee, sugar and the milk you have just brought in." Rebecca unpacked the shopping and all of it putting away into the walk in larder. Finding it would be a life saver in having a place to store all the shopping.

"Diana you've even bought me my favorite cakes."

"Rebecca I didn't buy them."

"She stood last night baking them all."

"Oh yes . "

"It not Thursday today is it ?"

"Yes so I had made them , well Thomas don't just sit there cut the cake."

"I would if I had a knife to cut it with."

"Hang on I'll get on for you Thomas." Carefully passing him a knife he cut the cake into slices. Time flew by as they drank their cups of tea. Eating the second slice of the delightful homemade cake the doorbell rang Rebecca looked at the clock it wasn't twelve so it couldn't be Daniel.

"Rebecca door."Putting her slice of cake down on the table she went to see who it could be. On opening it to her surprise it was Daniel friend Justin Hibbison. " Hi Just what are you doing here?"

" Oh Daniel had told me that he was moving his thing over here since all the cleaning had been done so though I'd come and give a hand to unpack."

" Well you better come on in as Daniel hasn't arrived yet." Just shutting the door behind her as the doorbell rang again. She opened the door. " Daniel "

" Oh you're ready then."

" What made you think I wouldn't be well darling you normally still in day at this time of day a sleep."

"Haha Daniel"

" Well don't just stand there let me in ."

"What time is it Thomas !!!!" She shouted through to the kitchen . "Twelve why it only Daniel at the door."

"Well darling don't just sit there go and give the lass a hand." Thomas said to Diana as Rebecca shouted for the two friends that could give her a helping hand. "Justin ,Diana come and give me a hand to unpack this van."The two friend headed straight towards the front door and out to the van. It didn't take them long to get everything out of the van.

As soon as the van was now totally unloaded Daniel paided Ian. "Heres the £30 as we agreed ."

"Thanks." Daniel had marked all the boxes as he packed them so they could be easily put into the correct rooms. So didn't take much for everything to be unpacked. " Glad your now here darling as I've missed you tons." As she quickly grabbed her first cuddle in a while.

"Well let me get everyone a cuppa." As Diana noticed they needed a minute to alone. At the table Justin and Thomas were busy trying to guess the age of the cottage. Even though Justin used to teach history at the local secondary school before retiring. He was finding it difficult to put his finger on the year that the cottage could of been built. Even after all the years he had know Daniel he'd never mentioned the fact the he was a retired history teacher. Till over hearing him say that the area's history had many connections with some of the local fairy tales. Also that there once was a enchanted manor house that had stood right where the cottage now stood.Immediately the question of her own family came to her mind as Justin's knowledge could help her research it. Even to find the truth out of the story she had grew up with.

"Justin you never told us that you used to teach history , is there any way you could help me research my family history?"

" Yes I could give it a go but I'm a bit rusty."

" Anyway would you like to stay for dinner "

"Yes if that ok!"

"Why yes as as you've helped unpack the heaviest items and placed them where they should be." Rebbeca and Diana now knew that they had a five to feed so started preparing it. It was also getting cold so Daniel and Thomas went into all the rooms down stairs and got them ready to just light. While the dinner was busy cooking the women got the table set in the beautiful dining room. The cutlery was the best silver set and her very best china dinner set. Two pm the dinner was ready to be served up Daniel had lit the fire in the dining room to get in warm through. Diana dished out two meals a time which Rebbeca carried through to dinner table where the three men were sitting waiting. The last two plates were Rebbeca and Diana's so they carried them through themselves. All were now seated at the table eating it suddenly felt as though time had rewound. As though they had been transported back to the victorian era. Rebecca looked around as she couldn't find a seat where she would of sat but this made her feel as though she wasn't to be there. Was this the start of the secret she was to find.

## Chapter three Bonds of friendship

The bond between the three friends had always strong to the extent they could be totally open with each other. Was this bond going to be strengthened further once the secrets of their family connection that had been hidden were discovered. Everyone had enjoyed the dinner and the stress of the day seemed to have vanished during the dinner. All the dishes were taken through to the kitchen by Justin ready for the two women to wash. As the men went through to the sitting room while the dishes were done giving the two friends time to talk. "Diana do you feel a thought you were not in the cottage but in the victorian servant's dining area?"

"Yes I did !!!"

" Diana a few weeks before your gave me the keys. I had dreamt that you had brought this cottage to thank me. Did you and Thomas buy here for that reason?"

"Yes we did it to thank you."

"Diana the cottage is enchanted ."

"How do you know that pet."

"Well with the answer that you've just given me has told me what I dreamt will all come true in one way or another."

"That also means both our family are some how connected to the house that justin had said used to stand here ."

"My grandmother had told me stories of a manor house which she had heard from her own mother's lips as a child."

"I also heard stories of a manor house from my Aunty Pearl. As she used to be s Nursing maid to the family there."

"Diana did you just say the name Pearl?"

"Yes Pearl and my mother Ruby."

"I saw both their ghosts in my dream."

"Darling Rebecca we have to find out the truth of those stories."

"Ok Diana but we'll keep this between us for now." Thomas knew it was getting late and it was an hour drive back to their house. "Diana its time to go!"

"OK I'm coming through."

"Justin would you like a lift ?"

"Yes please."

"Diana Justin getting a lift in our car."

"OK!" As they entered the room giving each other a hug and see you later .

"I'll ring you in a couple of days time."

" Ok speak to you then." Daniel had wondered what had kept them in the kitchen talking so long. As the dishes wouldn't have taken Rebbeca that long to get done. She didn't like to keep secrets from Daniel. As their relationship was built on trust from the day the first meet. But she had promised her friend to keep this one till they figured out what effects it would have on all of them.

Chapter four Childhood story.

As a child her grandmother had told her the stories of the Lord Marcus of Wishing Wells. How he had made his fortune by selling the goods he smuggled into the country after his trips abroad. the money he made he never wasted but used to help build and create a seaside town. Where the other sailing families could sell their own good that they brought legally into the country. This had brought peace and happiness to all that lived there. The way her grandmother told this part of the story alway made her think of the fairy tale of Dick Whittington. The only difference was that Marcus had been born aboard a trading ship.

When he had came of age to marry he married the love of his life. Isabella was her name. her beauty was unexplainable yet her hair was raven black, eye greener than the precious gem Jades and emerald combined. Her heart was pure gold as she could only see good in everyone she met. Those that had tried to do her harm ended up helping her do good things with in her power as the Lady of Wishing wells.

Marcus had a Manor house built on top of the cliff tops as soon as she had accepted his hand him marriage. She gave birth to a total of three beautiful children but only two of them were health when born. The youngest child had been pronounced dead when it was born. THe Year the poor child had been born a deadly disease had reached the shore line of the town. So Lady Isabella had given birth at home attended by a midwife. Marcus was away on urgent business in town to try to find a way to stop the spread of the disease.

He had unknowingly carried the disease and passed it onto Isabella when she fell pregnant. Without showing any symptoms of the disease she had thought that she'd escaped the disease and the pain that it inflicted on those that caught it. The disease had slightly affected the unborn child she carried. Until she gave birth to that child a beautiful baby girl. Who the midwife ordered to be removed as it had not made a sound or movement. A Nursing maid who had been brought up on a small farm had seen this many time with newborn lambs. Without delay she took the child out of the room to a room at the back of the house and did what she had seen her father do to the lambs. This brought life to child within seconds. Lady Isabella had been told that the child was dead as the Nursing Maid left the room. So the maid couldn't tell anyone of the fact the child was to live. Blaming herself for the death of the child Lady Isabella would not eat any food that was offered. This Weekend her health further as the disease slowly took hold of her life.

On arriving back from the town Marcus was given the new of his wife and the child from the Midwife who had attended her. He didn't want to lose his surviving children so ordered the staff to ensure that they were to not come in contact with their mother. But were to be entertained with things that brought them only pleasure. If they asked of their mother's where about the servant were to tell them that she was away on trips looking wonderful gifts to bring them on their birthdays. Right up till her death he had ensured that the children had came to believe this. When she died Marcus couldn't stand the sight of his childrens happy faces as it only brought him memories of their mothers death. Taking himself to a room in a local lodging house to protect them for his anger. As he knew they were not to be blamed for her death but himself as he had brought the disease to the manor house. He also thought that by taking himself to the lodging house he would be protecting them from the disease that had taken their mother. As he had started to show signs of the disease himself. He was stronger than their mother but when he had beaten the disease it was already too late for his children. When he received word that they were to dying he headed back to the manor house but arrived too late. The nursing maid that had save the child had seen him arrive to say his goodbye to his dying children. With the wish that she could tell him that she had not lasted all his children. Which would of gave him comfort of sorts. But in his face she saw anger that he had not been there for his children.

He entered the room the children bodies laid peacefully looking as though they were just sleeping. He knew that if there was to be anything good to come from this it would be to save the staff from caughting the disease so ordered all of them to leave the manor house. The nursing maid had know about the secret passage so took the child out of the house via that passage. This is where her grandmother always ended the story. But Rebbeca always wanted to know what had happened to the maid and child.

Chapter five Connections

Diana had told Rebecca that her Aunt Pearl was a Nursing maid and that her mother also worker in the manor house. Until the Lord Marcus of Wishing Wells had ordered all his staff to leave. But not what had happened after her mother and Aunt had left the Manor. Ruby was the older of the two sister. They had never kept secret from each other until the birth of the child. So a day before they had to leave the manor house Pearl knew she had to tell her sister of what she had done. Ruby had supported her little sister in everything they did. They planned that they would go their separate ways till she found a new employment and living quarters for the three of them. Ruby was able to find work within days of leaving the Manor house . As a Rich business man Harold Winterfall owned a grand house further down the coast had been looking for servant to work for him . As many of his old one had left his service as they had all worked till the were too old to work there anymore. So had moved into the village to live the rest of their day out. Most of the new staff were to live in the grand house but he also owned two small cottages on his land one his game keep the last of his original staff lived with his family. As Ruby had told him where they had last worked as servants at the Manor house . On this he knew that Ruby was telling the truth as Harold had heard of the plight of the Marcus of Wishing wells family and what the staff where like there. Therefore

Ruby and Pearl would by as loyal as they were to the marcus's family to him once they were employed. She had to find somewhere safe for the child that was in their care so with the other cottage being empty they could live they happily.

When the Harold's Of the house asked her where she would like to live she mentioned the cottage."Ruby can you please explain the reason why you would want to live there?"

"Sir I will be living there with my younger sister who is a young widow and has a small daughter to bring up her self. But she will also work alongside me in your household a servant if that is agreeable sir."

" Yes it is ."

"Don't just stand there go and fetch your sister and move into that cottage straight away lass." Pearl had been living in a small room in a derelict building in the town till Ruby had came to fetch her. Tell her how luck they were to have found a new employer and a new home to boot. " You always did had the brain big sister." was the first thing that she could think of saying.

On that she packed up her thing and wrapped the child warmly and the travelled back to the cottage and started to make more like a home. This ensured that the bond with child as she grew up was strong enough that no one would ever guess that the child was not her own. Pearl had named the child Issy as shortened version of the child's own mothers name. Each day she took Issy to the home of the gamekeeper where his wife looked after her while Pearl and Ruby went to work in the Grand house.

The gamekeepers children played with Issy after they had carried out their chore for their mother . So Issy was a happy child growing up along side her playmates. In the summer all the children were allowed to play in the grand house gardens as a treat. Without knowing that the Harold's Of the house didn't always go away in the summer. Then one summer that the three girls had lived in the cottage Issy was in the garden with her friends. As they had been given permission by the Harold as he enjoyed the sound of children playing . He had stayed at home every year but didn't leave the house but went to his study in the north facing rooms. Just so he could hear the children playing as it brought him a sense of being a child again. As he looked outside there he caught his first glimpse of Issy playing. Instantly he knew that Pearl was not the child's natural mother, but knew who was. He had to hear the truth from Pearl lips before doing anything. "Dick my man." Dick was his personal butler and loyal servant.

"Yes sir."

"Good and tell that servant girl called Pearl I require her to come to my room as I need to speak to her." All Harold's servants had know through their own experience that when the master of the household asked for you to go to his private rooms its was serious. Mean that you were either going to be promoted or given marching orders to leave the household. As the only other person who had free access to that area was Dick Harold's butler. " Dick can you tell me why he has asked for me?"

" No mama." If he had said anything other than his orders he would of been given his own marching orders. They reached the door and Dick knocked twice.

"Come in Pearl."On those word Dick opened the door for her .

"Yes sir"

"That all Dick my man for now."

"Take a seat Pearl." She sat on the couch nearest the desk. Harold walked towards the couch and sat next to her so her could look straight into her eyes to see if she was going to lie to him or tell the full truth.

"Don't worry lass you're not in trouble yet."

"Sir you ordered me to come here sir ."

"Yes I did Pearl , you've proven to be a hard worker from the day you arrived . Even looking after a child that isn't even your own."

"What are you say ?"

"Pearl that child is not your daughter is she?"

"She's the only surviving child of Marcus of Wishing Wells."

"I thought so as she has her mother beauty."

"But Pearl how come she come into your car. "

"Sir it a long story but allow me to tell you."

"OK tell me." Telling of how the poor child was pronounced dead at her birth but she save the child life . This took a full hour but he listened without interrupting her once.

" What do you intend to do sir?"

" Every thing in my power to ensure your life and the child you have named Issy are given the best life I can provide for without your secret being discovered by the rest of the staff . That is until she is at the age to understand what we have done to protect her . Which I will leave up to you. "

" Oh sir thank you as it will make my life much easier ."

" Starting from tonight by putting in place the order that your are to be treat as though you and Issy were always members of my family which had not been know of till to day. Issy is to go to the best boarding school when she is old enough . I will till then teach her myself in my study. As for the problem of your sister that is where my own secret comes into play."

"What could that secret be?"

"We've fallen in love and have been for many years secretly meeting in a place that only one member of my staff here is aware of."

" So you mean that dick your servant knew of this and that you're planning to ask her for her hand in marriage?"

"Yes I do intend to make a honest woman of her now."

"What about living quarter for Issy and myself as you're going to tell the staff we're family."

"Your both to move into the east wing of this house as it only right for her due to her true position in society."

"When do you mean to ask my sister then?"

"I'll ask her later this month."

"May I now leave future brother-in-law.

"Yes you may future sister-in-law."

"Should I get Dick to give the order for the rest of the staff to gather in the main hall."

"Yes and Pearl my name is Harold so please call me that from this day on." Ruby and Harold were married in the family chapel a year later. Pearls time as a servant had ended that night but her friendship with the staff of the house never changed. Until she left the house and married a tradesman who lived in the village. Issy then was placed into Rubies and Harold capable hands. She still visited the grand house each summer to see her sister and new niece Diana also to ensure that Issy was happy. Issy had became to be treat as though she was a true member of the family right up till her own death. Diana always remembered those happy days. Her Aunt Pearl had told her the truth of Issys true family. But Diana only loved Issy even more after hearing the story. Pearl had told her that till the day she died Issy was not to find out the truth. But she was to receive a letter from Pearl for the both of them on which was addressed to Issy held the truth to be given to her .

Chapter six Secrets now to be told.

Two day had passed since saying goodbye to Diana. The look on Dianas face still lingered in Rebecca's eyes. Trying not to worry she busied herself. The phone rang and automatically Rebecca picked up the phone. "HI Diana."

"Hi Rebecca can you please come over ?"

"Why?"

"I've found a parcel and you need to see it for yourself."

"You sound worried."

"Rebbeca what you will see will change things between us."

"Diana what do you mean?"

"Just come over and bring Daniel, Justin."

"OK what time ?"

"Oh say three as normal."

"Are you ok though."

"Yes and No."

"See you at three and don't worry." Diana had already put down the phone by the time she had finished the sentence. Normally Rebecca would visit Diana and Thomas alone. Yet her friend had requested her to take Daniel and Justin along. Daniel could chat with Thomas as they both loved gardening. But Justin was she going to ask him piece together her story and the what the parcel had in it. Inside that parcel there was two letters one addressed to her and one to Issy. But also other items which diana had forgotten all about till her friend had mentioned her Aunts name. As she had been given it some years ago and she had not wanted to open it till she had found Issy. But Issy had died before she could find her to give the letter to her. So she had locked it away in a chest forgotten but when she got back home and Thomas was watching television she went to her spare room where she stored all her personal memory boxes in a large wooden chest that was lockable and she was the only one to have a key to it on a chain she wore. Going straight to the chest she opened the lock and lifted the parcel then took it into her bedroom. Opening it carefully and pulled out the letters one by one. Taking her one in her hand peeling the top away so not to rip what may be inside. The letter as she read it was from her aunt Pearl. Rebecca had to read this for herself as it would prove that Rebecca's grandmother was trying to pass down the truth of the families history.

It only took half an hour to reach her friends house."Diana's been cooking her cakes again."

"How do you know that darling Rebecca?"

"I can smell them in the air a I always smell them on a Thursday." Diana opened the door giving them a warm welcoming hug. "Daniel Thomas is throwing the sitting room and looking forward in talking to your about our garden. "OK."

"Thomas I bring a pot of tea and some of my cake through in a bit."

"Us men will be Ok!"

"Rebecca , Justin come into my kitchen we can talk there." Putting the kettle on as Justin and Rebecca sat down at the table. "Diana is this that your wanted me to look at?"

"Yes that parcel."

"But why could you not talk about on the phone?"

"Right now let me get everyone a cup of tea and slice of my home made cake that you enjoy."

"Can I help you then?"

"Yes you know where my best china cups are and the ones we use, get two of the best for Justin and Daniel.

"Are the tea tray in the same place?"

"Yes and can you pour our three cups of tea out."

"Are you talking THomas and Daniels through for them?"

"Yes then I'll come and sit down next to you."This Diana had done within two seconds as she was used to having visitors.

"Right that the parcel but I wanted to be with you face to face as I tell you about the parcel."

"So why are you so worried?" Diana couldn't answer straight away but asked Justin a question about the area's history. "You know the history of the area Justin?

"Yes but please tell me how that helps any?"

"Just tell if what I'm about to say is true ."

"OK Diana!"

"Once there was a Lord Marcus of Wishing Wells who had a Manor house up the coast from here in fact right where the cottage is ."

"Yes but that house was burnt down in a fire."

"Rebbeca open the parcel please."

" Its addressed to you and someone called Issy Winter Falls."

"Rebbeca just open it please." Starting to cry as Rebecca opened the parcel .

"Diana what does this have to do with what you have just asked me?"

"Justin in the gardens of that house there should of had a total of five graves but there is only three."

"Rebecca what's in that parcel with the two letters pet?"

"Diana one of the letters had Isabella wrote on it."

"Isn't Issy short for Isabella,Rebecca."

"Yes !"

" Justin you looked shock at the fact that I know there should've been five graves don't be."

"Thomas grandfather Jacob Bellado was the head gardener at the manor house and many other big houses along the coast. And when the Lady of wishing wells died weeks after giving birth to her youngest child . Yes the local legend as it is told the child was supposed to have been pronounced dead when born. Except when my Aunty Pearl had brought the child back to life. But when the other two children died month later Jacob had been ordered to bury them in the gardens as that where they were the happiest. Within a short time after Marcus ordered all of his staff to leave the Manor. As he had given the ownership of the house to his wifes surviving relatives. "But who burnt the house down?"

"It had been said it was a freak accident. the truth Justin and Rebecca was that in grief the Marcus had sneaked back into the house via the smugglers passage and started the fire."

"Yet there was no bodies found in the ashes."

"Diana in my grandmother's story she had mentioned that a foreign sailor once turned up at my Great great grandmothers house. Even left gifts for her daughter. She only remembered this part before she took ill."

" The family that lived there after Marcus could've been away on business and he could of escapes back down the passage Justin."

"Yes as it was built to his own instructions."

" But who is Issy and how does this all connect to her?"

"She's the surviving daughter of the Wishing Wells family."

" The Lord Marcus surely was told of her death Diana?"

" He was told exactly that the day she was born. So after the older children had died he had nothing to stay for."

"Diana there a photo of your and a little girl older than you by the looks of her. "

"Rebbeca that photo is of me and Issy." Justin wanted to try and figure out when the the photo had been taken so had asked to see it. Looking at every detail he notice something. "Diana that was taken thirteen years after records of the manor house fire, but who is that standing in the back ground?

"Rebecca Issy looks like you."

"No way let me look again." As Justin was handing it back to Rebecca he noticed that it had another on stuck to its back. "Turn the photo over as there is another one on the back."

"Diana on this one Issy is my age."

"Justin take another look and tell there is not similarities."

" Rebbeca it like a mirror image of you."

"Rebbeca what was your great grandmother's name?"

" I think Bella!"

"Diana is Bella another version of Isabella."

" Rebbeca Your Issy Great granddaughter."

"What I can't be!"

" Rebbeca that house is your ancestral home."

" DIANA

"REBECCA NIECE."

"Justin please tell me how can this be."

"Rebecca I can't but lets look at the other letter." Daniel and Thomas had heard the two women crying. This made them want to find out what was going on and to see that the women they loved were ok went straight to the kitchen. "Lad s take a seat as what you are about to hear will shock you both."

"You've heard me tell you that my Aunty Pearl was a Nursing maid but till not I hadn't told anyone that she was the one that rescued the last known member of the Wishing wells family know by those that grew up with her as Issy. Yes Thomas the little girl I grew up with as my older sister was really that person. My parent had always know the truth also. This didn't affect the way they loved us both. Until the day my father died everything was peaceful. That night my mother and Issy had argued over her true rights to what he had left in his will to the both of us. In anger my mother told her that he wasn't even her real father and she wasn't her real mother. This hurt Issy so much that she packed her belonging and walked out. I never stopped wondering what had happened to her . Even hoping that one day she would walk back through those doors. If not that she had made a good life for herself . Then one day after my mother died I received a letter saying that she had died. I was supposed to have given her that letter the day my aunt died, as I couldn't find her I wasn't able to. I loved like a sister even though my aunt had told me when I was young who she really was but to my mind she was just my big sister to me.So Rebecca in my eyes you're my niece even if in blood you're still a relative." Thomas look at both of them in shock but with a smile on his face.

" Rebbeca don't just sit there you've every right to open that other letter."

"Good Darling I'm right here."

"Is that ok Diana."

"Rebbeca its Yours open it."

Dear Issy,

When you receive this please forgive me of keep this secret from you till my death. As my love for you is as a mother would love her own child but your not my child. Your true name is Isabella of Wishing wells. You were pronounced dead when your were born but I brought you back to life. And keep you safe from the disease that took you poor mothers life and also your older siblings a month later.

I Pearl Granger looked after you as though you were my own without your father knowledge as he was grieving the deaths I've mentioned earlier in this letter and would of killed you in a fit of anger if he had know that you were still alive as your mother had given up the fight for her life once she had been told by the midwife who delivered you that you were dead. I had wanted to let him know that you were alive when your sister and brother had died. I LOVED YOU as my own and left you with my sister and her husband to bring you up as your true position in society being higher than what i could provide standard of living for .But I never stopped loving you. Diana has also loved you as though you were her own sister and will always love you that way.

Faithfully

Aunty Pearl Granger

"Diana what did your letter say ."

"Nothing that I didn't already know except that the letter you have just read was to be given to Issy."

"Diana is there anything else in that parcel?"

"Yes two gold lockets Justin."

"Here you are pet this ones yours."

Rebecca opened it to find inside there was a small key.

" Daniel in the cottage in the sitting room theres a large picture hanging next to the fireplace."

"Yes is there a small key hole?"

" Rebbeca don't do anything till I visit you next week promise."

"Yes aunty diana." As they all started laughing .

"Well leave it for now and say our goodbyes."

"Yes it getting late and you have to get back to the cottage so Daniel can take his evening medication."

Rebecca walked over to Diana and gave her the biggest hug she could give. As she headed to front door followed by daniel who was busy talking to Thomas and Justin was trying to get his attention to tell him that she was already at the front door.

But what would the key unlock"!!!!!!!!]

Printed in Great Britain
by Amazon